W9-BDK-703

My Friend Rabbit

ERIC ROHMANN

SCHOLASTIC INC.

New York   Toronto   London   Auckland   Sydney
Mexico City   New Delhi   Hong Kong   Buenos Aires

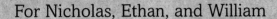

For Nicholas, Ethan, and William

No part of this publication may be reproduced, stored in a retrieval system, or transmitted in any form or by any means, electronic, mechanical, photocopying, recording, or otherwise, without written permission of the publisher. For information regarding permission, write to Roaring Brook Press, a division of The Millbrook Press, 2 Old Milford Road, Brookfield, Connecticut 06084.

ISBN 0-439-57820-5

Copyright © 2002 by Eric Rohmann. All rights reserved. Published by Scholastic Inc., 557 Broadway, New York, NY 10012, by arrangement with Roaring Brook Press, a division of The Millbrook Press. SCHOLASTIC and associated logos are trademarks and/or registered trademarks of Scholastic Inc.

12 11 10 9   8 9/0

Printed in the U.S.A.   40

First Scholastic paperback printing, October 2004

My friend Rabbit means well.
But whatever he does,
wherever he goes,

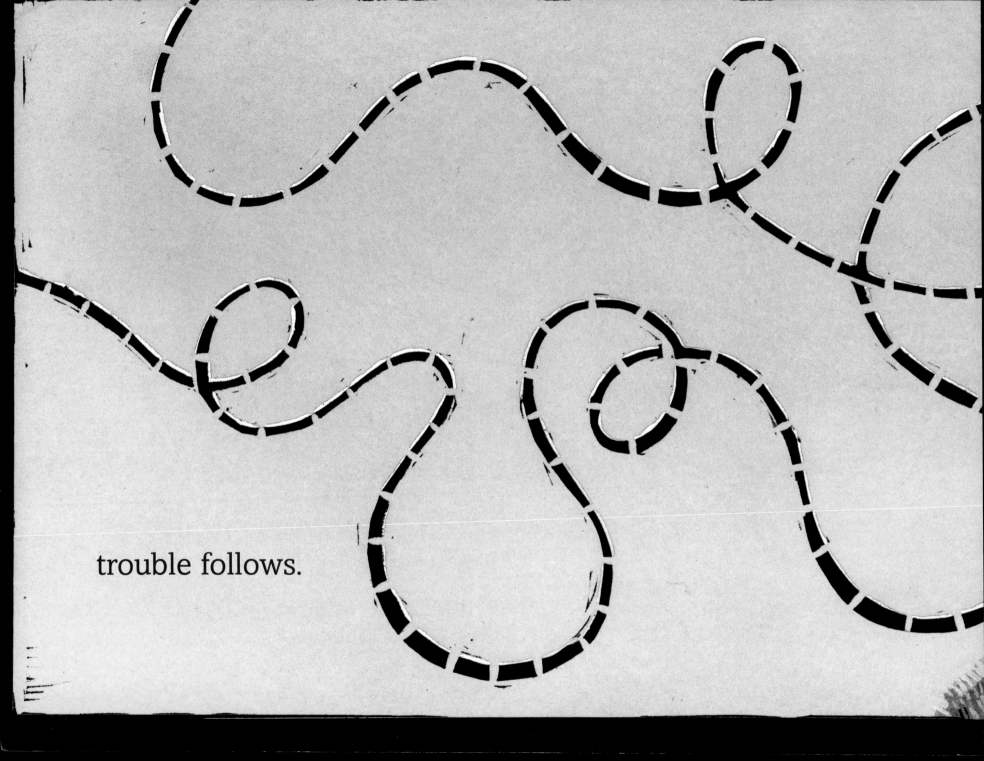

trouble follows.

"Not to worry, Mouse. I've got an idea!"

The plane was
just out of reach.
Rabbit said,
'Not to worry,
Mouse, I've
got an idea."

So Rabbit held Squirrel
and Squirrel held me . . .

but then . . .

The animals
were not
happy.

But Rabbit means well.

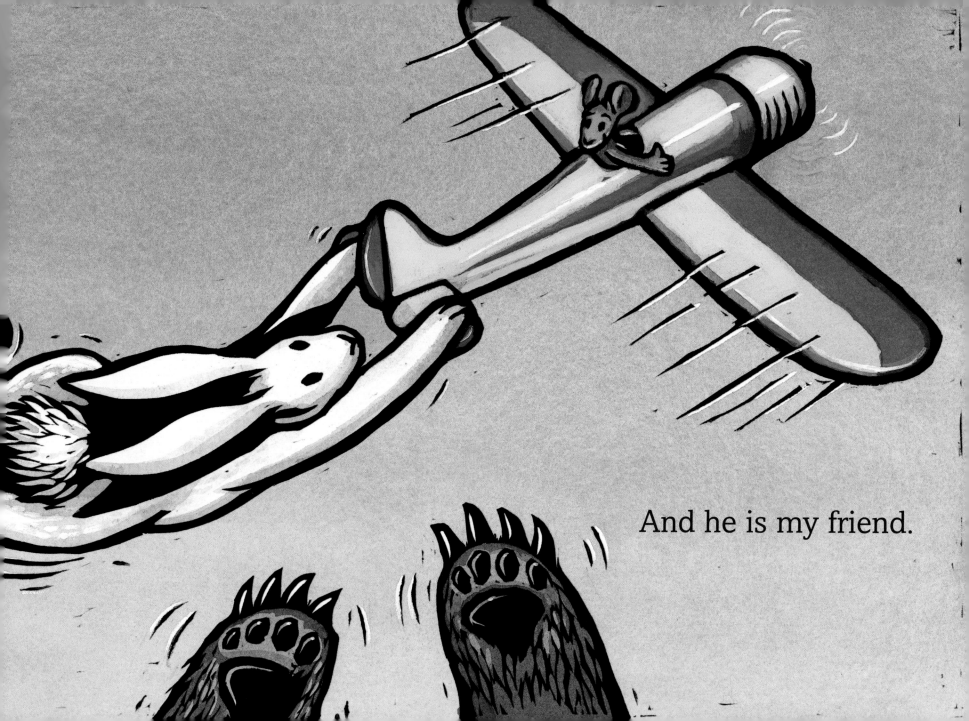

And he is my friend.

Even if, whatever he does,

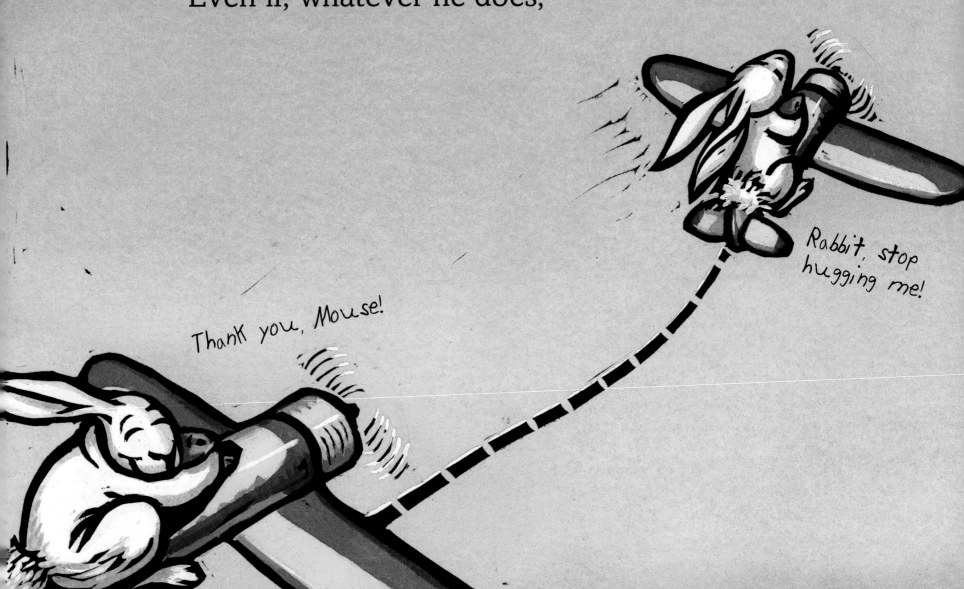

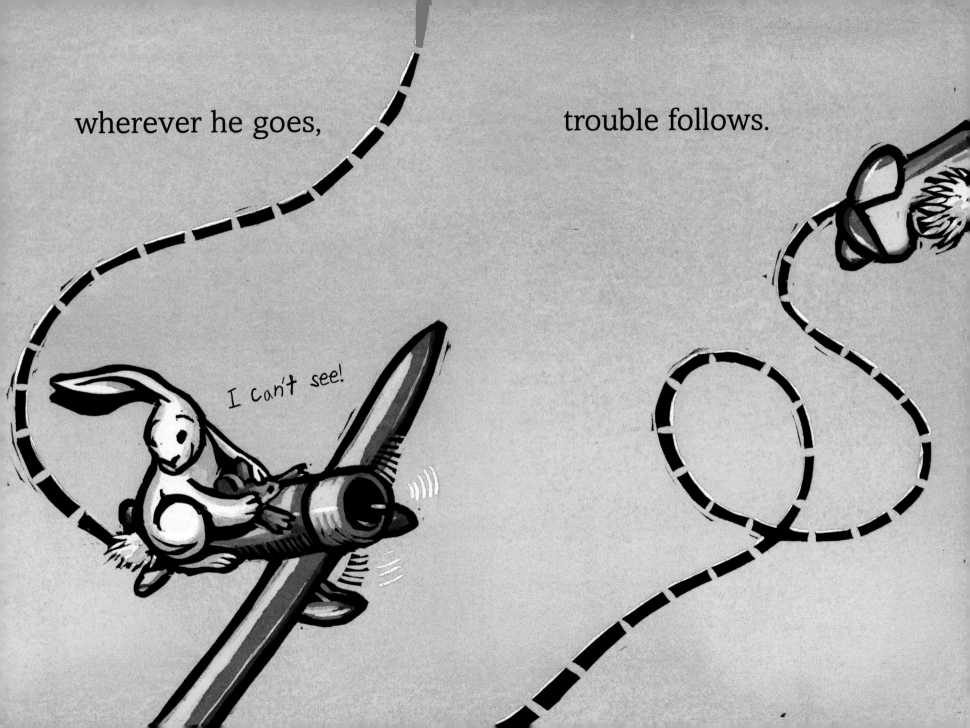

"Not to worry, Mouse,
    I've got an idea."